# SHADOW LIGHT

## WITCH ACADEMY OF ASHES

R.L. WILSON

Cover Designer: Charmaine Ross

Editing: Rainlyt Editing

Proof Reader: Cassie Hess-Dean

Formatting: R.L. Wilson

R.L.Wilson Shadow Light, The Witch Academy of Ashes, Book Two March 2021 R. L.Wilson/Exquisite Novelty Publishing LLC

 Created with Vellum

*Thank you for purchasing Shadow Light*

*Thank you to all my supporters, friends, Arc group, and beta readers for encouraging me, even on the days when I wanted to throw the towel in.*

*Special thanks to my many mentors. Your mentorship is invaluable. You kept me motivated, gave me advice, and never asked for anything in return. The world needs more people like you.*

*Special thanks to my husband and kids who stayed up late listening to my ideas and being alpha readers. I hope to make you guys proud of me.*

*Last but not Least I have to thank God for giving me the strength and the courage to keep striving.*

R.L.Wilson

# FREE BOOK

Check out my website and claim your free book
www.rlwilsonauthor.com

Or signup for my newsletter:
https://www.subscribepage.com/f2v6g5

# BLURB

**Jail is the last place I thought I'd end up. Yet here
I am**

Now my only goal is to get out of this filthy place
full of degenerates and track down the actual killer.

With rage fueling my every move and my friends,
Kenny, James, and his twin brother Josh by my side. I
know I'll find Prince, the dark fae, and get my life
back.

This is.. if all go as planned. If not, I might never get
to live the life of a teenage girl and I'll definitely
never attend another party.

Find Prince and don't fall in love with him. How hard could that be. How hard could that be?

I'm about to find out.

**Scroll up and take ONE CLICK to start this magical journey.**

I'm nobody's criminal, but they are hauling me to jail. I can always tell when they have a guilty conscious: they stay silent. I'm too tired to fight with the officer driving the squad car. My face stings with pain, my eye is swollen. It's clear I'm the victim.

"Officer, can you tell me why I'm being arrested?"

He refuses to answer my questions, but sadly, I think the headmaster called the police on me. I can't believe this shit. I grimace as my bruised face throbs with pain.

Maybe I will get a phone call. I could call Grace. Other than that, I have no one else to call. I don't think Mother has a phone. There's no way for me to contact her. Not that she could help me anyway.

She's been in jail a time or two herself, and no one helped her out either.

A thick tension clouds the small space in this car like a foul odor. The officer looks at me through the rearview mirror. His thick lips part as if he wants to speak, but he snatches his eyes from the mirror and continues driving. He says nothing, leaving me in the dark. I'm sure he knows about this conspiracy going on.

The ride to the police station is a short one. It's only two city blocks. The front entrance of campus. I must convince him to tell me something before we arrive at the station. Unless he's involved in this coverup.

I'm much too pretty to be in prison. From what I've seen on television, the butch women like pretty girls like me. I can hold my own against most girls my size, but I don't know my magic well enough to fight off muscular, built women.

"Can you tell me anything?" I growl.

"No, they instructed me to take you straight to the station," he grunts. "You'll find out what the charges are soon."

"Charges?" My mouth becomes dry. "I'm telling you I didn't do shit."

"There are three sides to a story. Your side, the

other person's side, and somewhere in the middle lies the truth." He scratches his head, moving the bronze hair to one side. "That's where law enforcement comes in: to find the truth," he barks.

Those are the most words he has spoken all day. The car comes to a stall and I flick a stare at the police station. I'd promise myself after seeing Mother in prison that I'd never go to prison. The place steals the blood from you. Mother lost her appetite for life there. Her color disappeared along with her weight. She was never the same. I can only imagine the horrors she must have faced there. I must find a way out.

"Let's go," he says. Every nerve in my body fires to propel myself toward the door. Forcing myself out the squad car, I take a hard swallow, then hobble toward the entrance. My hands cuffed tightly behind my back make me appear to be a hardened criminal. I came here yesterday as a visitor and today as a prisoner.

I feel like I'm taking my last walk toward the electric chair. The harsh stares from my peers make me cringe. I want to hide in the corner or disappear altogether. Most students come here for parking passes or to pay tickets, not in handcuffs.

The officer ushers me to the back of the precinct.

I assumed I'd be thrown to the wolves in a tiny cell; I got it all wrong. He put me in an empty room. There's nothing but a desk and chair with white brick walls, the kind you would see in a mental institution, not a pristine supernatural academy. There's also a large glass window. I've seen enough Law and Order to know that they are recording me.

There's no need for them to record me. I'm not saying shit. But I am innocent. I've grown weary of saying who the culprit is. He seems to slither his way out of out every situation like a slippery weasel.

The officer exits the room as a lady enters. She's sporting a blonde wig that covers her forehead, only revealing her sinister eyes. Let me guess, I'm supposed to confess to her. Get the fuck out of here.

She takes a seat, exposing her gun in a holster on her hip. She isn't wearing a uniform. I guess she's a detective. She needs to do her damn job and find Prince. He committed murder and an assault.

"Hello, I'm Maggie. I'll be asking you a few questions," she says. Her red lipstick left stains on her teeth. I want to tell her, but I'll keep quiet.

"Hi."

"Are you Ronielle Simms?"

Suppressing an eye roll, I sigh. "That would be me." It's irritating. She knows my name.

"I need to inform you everything here is being recorded."

She didn't need to tell me. I'm no idiot. I have little to say, anyway.

"Can you get me out of these cuffs? They hurt." I frown.

"Sure." She rises from the chair. The clack of her heels pierces my ears. She releases me my from my shackles. I rub my wrists as they throb in pain. The red rings around my wrists are hideous. *It will be over faster the more cooperative I am,* I think.

She swoops her hair to the side as she sashays back to her chair. She better not move it too much. I'm sure she will be embarrassed if it comes off. I know it's a wig. Grandma had a room filled with wigs.

Her eyes flicker. She is supernatural, I can tell. She has a magical aura surrounding her. But I can tell she thinks she's the cat's meow. She has on a ton of makeup and her wrist is laced with silver bracelets. I don't see a wedding ring, though. It all makes sense. She's looking for a husband. Not going to find one in a jail, I hope.

"Let's cut to the chase," she says.

"Let's," I respond, raising a brow.

"We have a lot of evidence to suggest that you harmed someone."

I shoot a disgusted frown at her. "What are you talking about? Don't you see my face?"

"Your dorm room is covered in blood. It covers the walls and the floor."

"Yeah, I told you he attacked me," I yell. No one is listening to me.

"You only have a few minor scratches and bruises. Nothing to justify the large puddle of blood in your room."

Heaviness takes over my breathing. I gasp for air as she talks. What the hell is she getting at?

"Where is the body?" she asks.

"Body? What body? Prince is the killer," I plead. "I didn't kill anyone. He attacked me. That's my blood in there."

"Now is the time to be honest." Her tone lowers, even calmer than before. "I can help you. Maybe it was a mistake." She grabs the mug from her desk and takes a sip, never taking her eyes off me.

Oh, she's trying to mind-fuck me. "No, I didn't make any mistakes."

"Crime investigators are there now, getting samples of the blood. By tomorrow we will know who the blood belongs to."

"Great. Meanwhile, you should go search for Prince."

"Who is this Prince? What's his last name?"

"I don't know his last name, but he attacked me."

"The problem with that story is no one knows or has seen this Prince. Do yourself a favor: confess, so you don't get life."

The stare I shoot at her should have cut her face. I'm too angry to speak. My blood is boiling.

"Fine, have it your way. Officer!" she yells. The door unlocks. The officer steps into the room. His eyes brighten at the sight of her. "Take her to a cell." She gives me a look of disgust.

Oh, this shit is getting real. How do I escape this nightmare?

2

I'm ushered down the dreaded hall and thrown into one of the four cells. "Wait," I scream before he closes the bar. "This is not a women's cell."

"This is the holding cell," he grunts. "Everything is co-ed here." He locks the door. "When you leave, you're either going home or to prison."

Prison. The word I never wanted to hear associated with my name. My mangled screams are trapped somewhere in my throat. I shudder back and flip a quick glance at the twin boys sitting on the steel benches. Identical twins, at that. The high-pitched echoes of the guard walking away, leaving me alone with two males, leaves me in shock.

I pace the floor. Finally, I take a seat on the bench

opposite of the twins. I can't believe they integrate males and females in the same cell. Lowering my head, I bury it in my hands. I take in a heady breath, trying to prevent the tears filling my eyes from falling. I don't want to appear weak, but I'm scared as hell.

"Everything will be okay," a raspy voice says. I nod in agreement, but I don't bother looking at them. They have no idea why I'm here. They can't assure me everything will be okay.

"Miss, don't worry."

I narrow my guess in on the twins. "What?" I question, sniffling.

"Don't worry. You're much too pretty to be angry."

I grin. It's the first time I've smiled today. They are gorgeous guys, I must admit. I'm mad, not blind. "Hi. I'm Ronielle, but everyone calls me Ronnie."

"See, I knew you had a friendly spirit. I've gained a sixth sense for energy. I'm Josh, and this is my brother, James. We're twins," they both respond.

"I can see that." I chuckle.

"What did a pretty girl like you do to get thrown in here with wolves?" James questions.

I can tell them apart now. James has an orange shirt and Josh has on a blue shirt. But everything else, including their jeans, are identical. James also has pink pupils. The longer I stare, the more dangerous it is. I'm mesmerized by his eyes. Knowing I have a boyfriend puts me in a sticky situation.

"I got falsely accused of something I didn't do."

"That's weird," James says. "So did we. Did office Vincent arrest you?"

"Who?"

"Officer Vincent from campus police." He raises his hand, showing height level. "Tall, stocky, hardly ever says anything."

"Yeah. That would be the one."

"It's likely they don't have any factual evidence. They arrested us because we threatened to go public with a campus secret."

The screech of the bars opening makes my body tense all over. I don't turn around to see the guard until I hear my name. "Ronielle." My stomach drops. The smooth voice is like music to my ears.

It's Kenneth. I shift around, and my gaze lands on his handsome face. I blink several times to be sure I'm not hallucinating. I thought they would never let me see him. He rushes to my side. I touch his chest and it feels like holding a million dollars in my hand.

I burry my head in his chest. "They must let me out," I plead.

"Calm down. It's okay. I'll make sure you get out of here. What happened?" he whispers.

"I tried telling you before. Prince, he's the killer." A jolt of rage pumps through my blood when I speak the name Prince.

"Ronielle, I told you to leave that alone. I can handle myself in here."

I shake my head. Tears form and roll down my cheeks. I say nothing. He came looking for me.

"What?" he says, anger shooting across his face.

"Prince. He came to my dorm room and attacked me." I roll up my sweater, showing my many bruises and scratches. I then turn my face so he can see my bruised cheek.

He drives his left fist into his hand. "Mother fucker!" he yells. "Don't worry. I'll get you out of here." That brings some peace to me, though I don't know how he'll achieve that goal.

The guard stands at the bars, looking down at his watch, then clears his throat. "I have to go. I'll come back when I can," Kenneth says. He stands and I grip his hand. "It's okay, Ronnie. No one here will lay a finger on you." He glares at the twins with an expression of "I dare you".

As he leaves, I suddenly feel as if I'm disappearing through the cracks in the concrete. Parts of me are drifting away. A claustrophobic sensation wears me down.

"Kenneth is your boyfriend?" one of them asks. I suddenly become aware of my surroundings. I almost forgot they were in this cell with me. I was only thinking about Kenny, about how wonderful it would be if we both walked out of this shit hole, together.

"Yes, why?" I respond.

"We think you could do much better," Josh says.

I glare at him. "What wrong with Kenny?" I growl.

"Nothing. He just has quite the reputation." His eyes bulge. "Of being a ladies' man. He has sprinkled a little of his magic on you."

"No, it's not like that. I don't care about his past. All I care about is the present and how he treats me."

"Fair enough," James says, holding his hands up.

"What are you exposing about the school?"

"Well, we couldn't help but overhear you talking about Prince with your boyfriend. I guess we all have something in common," Josh says.

A confused look forms on my face.

"Prince is who were exposing. And the cover-up by the school," James barks.

Cover up. I knew there was something fishy about this whole situation. The officer says they never heard of a Prince. Bullshit.

"Prince is a dark fae, as we both are. But he has been feeding off female students for years. No one is doing anything about it."

"That's what happened to my friend. They found her in her room dead, her body turning to ash. He had sucked the life from her."

A look of dread creeps upon both of their faces. "We must get out too."

"What's wrong?" I question.

"Our sister came up missing. We are certain that Prince kidnapped her. He usually feeds on them for a few days or weeks, sucking the life out of them."

Something must have gone wrong with Shelly. I'm sure she tried fighting for her life. That must be the reason there were bite marks on her neck.

"We have to save our sister. We go to Mage Academy, and Natalie, our sister, goes to Supernatural Academy," Josh expels.

"I can't tell our parents we let our little sister out of our sight," James insists.

"How long has she been missing?" I question.

"Two days," Josh says.

"Maybe you can ask your boyfriend to get us out too," James says.

"I can ask," I respond, grimacing. I'm uncertain that Kenneth can get me out, much less two other people.

There is something dark happening on this campus and I plan to bust the case wide open.

3

———————

disgruntled voice slices through the air, shouting in rage. I can't force my eyes open. A bad dream, I suppose. I reposition myself and continue sleeping. The voice sounds again. It's not Grace's voice. It's a tenor voice, a male voice. A constant ache in my back and the scent of coffee forces me awake. I let out a yawn. I open my eyes only to realize I'm still alive and in fucking jail. I jump up. What the fuck? Damn, I'm still in here. The wild insults and vulgar language carry down the hall.

"Officer," I yell.

I dart my gaze over to the twins. They are sleeping on the same bench. One is turns around from the sound of my yelling. I scan the surroundings, feeling pity for myself. How did I end up inside a cell with brick walls? I'm caged like a damn animal. Grandmother would turn in her grave if she knew.

The guard comes striding toward the cell. I'm grateful it's a female. Female guards are less aggressive than the male guards. Maybe she'll have some pity for me and fetch me a decent meal. Something better than the slop they fed us last night. However, she brings plenty of sass with her.

"I have to use the ladies' room," I bark.

"There's a toilet over there." She points to the nasty toilet sitting in the corner.

I'm sure as fuck not using that toilet. They haven't cleaned it in so long it turned brown.

"No, I won't be using that bathroom. Besides, you have me in here with two boys."

She glances at the toilet and frowns in the disgust, then pulls the key from the ring on her hip and unlocks the bars. The clink of the bars opening gave me some hope. I don't need to reenter the cage. My feet are stiff and numb, causing a sharp pain every time my feet pound into the concrete floor.

The reality of the inhumane living conditions ignite sheer horrid within me. I have lived in some unimaginable living conditions, but nothing this filthy.

"Here you go," she says. The woman in her radiating. She hands me a small box. "They will bring you guys some breakfast soon."

"What time is it?" I ask while rifling through the box. A tooth brush, a face towel, a small bar of soap, and toothpaste. The sample size like you get at the hotels.

"7:15."

"Thanks," I say as I head to the bathroom. *It's Wednesday,* I think. My first class starts at 9:30. I must be released soon.

I get to the bathroom and a sigh of relief escapes my lips. It's clean, with a fresh scent and a toilet free from stains. Must be the employees' bathroom. I don't understand why the prisoners' cell is so nasty. But I guess if you go to prison no one cares how you live.

I flip on the water. Steam dances from the sink. Piping hot water, just the way I like it. I run the water on the towel, then place it on my face. It brings tears to my eyes. How did I end up in jail? I flip a glance to the small window in the corner. I race over only to see the sun rising. The window is covered by bars on the outside. An icy chill moves down my back. There's no way out.

I finish my self-care and make my way back to the cell. The twins are awake now and eating breakfast. Someone had sat a tray for me on the bench I was sleeping on. This what they call breakfast. A patty of mystery meat that resembles cat food, toast with no jelly, and eggs. I have to eat something. Guess these eggs will be breakfast. I grab the plastic fork and take a bite. Damn, the eggs aren't even real.

I take a quick glance at the twins and notice that they are chowing down. As if this isn't the worst food they have ever seen. Josh gives me a dangerous stare. He appears grim, as if he has bad news. My heart suddenly flickers. He wants to say something, but he doesn't know how. I'm afraid of his thoughts. I don't need any slanderous news. The twins have given me enough of a scandal for a lifetime.

"What is it?" I ask. My mind won't stop racing until I'm informed.

James looks at me as if he was caught cheating on a test. Josh keeps his mouth sealed, but he is the one who is more assertive. Talking with them yesterday had given me a glimpse into their souls.

Whatever news they have, I'm sure they are keeping quiet to spare my feelings.

I have a soft spot for them both. Ok, maybe it's more of a sexual desire. I can't understand how I can imagine the twins sexually, the way I view Kenny. Sure, I see guys and think they're handsome. I've never wanted to know them on an intimate level. But it's like I have known these men a lifetime. Their fears, how much they love their sister. We talked all night, nearly.

"Josh, what is it?"

"It's your boyfriend."

"What about Kenny?" I question with a snarl.

He looks up at the ceiling, avoiding eye contact. "Rumor has it he takes females to Prince." He shoots me a sharp stare while pushing his tray aside. "To feed off."

I pause and give the stare of death. "That's a damn lie. Kenny wouldn't do anything like that."

Especially not to Shelly. "Who told you guys that?"

"It's just a rumor," James explains. "Maybe there's no truth to it."

The guard bangs on the bars. "Ronielle, Kenneth has requested you," she says.

I have mixed emotions. The twins and this horrendous rumor are giving me palpitations. A slight bit of doubt about Kenny invades my mind. I push that doubt deep to the back of my mind. I flick a glance at the twins.

Then I follow the guard down the hall to another cell. Kenny's face fills with passion at the sight of me.

All I see is a loving soul, someone I know who loves me. He's not this monster everyone is painting him to be.

The guard opens the cell, and I enter. The cell is filled with twenty people. Kenny gets special privileges here, but I'm not sure why.

He places his lips on mine and gives me a hug. "You will be released within the hour. You must get to class, right?" He smiles.

"Yeah, what about you?"

"Don't worry about me." He kisses me on the forehead. "I'll be out of here when it's my time. But you..." He grimaces and the vein in his forehead protrudes. "Promise me you will leave this alone. It can only cause you harm."

The thought of him working with Prince swims through my head. I know him better than that. I won't dare ask such a frivolous question.

"One tiny request."

"Sure. Anything."

"Can you help the twins too?"

"What? No. I can't help everybody."

"But they're in for a stupid reason: searching into the same case." I gaze into his brown eyes. "Their sister is missing."

"Is that right? What happen to their sister?"

"She was kidnapped."

"I'll see what I can do. But I'm not making any promises."

I wrap my arms around him and kiss him on the cheek. "Thank you," I whisper.

"Time is up," the guards growls,

"I'll call you tonight," Kenny says before I exit the cell.

Finally, I'm free. I said I'd leave the case alone. Once this case is closed and Prince is in jail, I'll stop snooping. But I need the help of the twins. With their help, we can take down Prince.

4

You would think that I would go straight to Prince's house, curse him for being the asshole that he is. Maybe use my strength of being a witch to my advantage.

He is a mage. He's taller, bigger, and stronger. And I haven't quite tapped into all the magic I have.

I get home with enough time to shower and grab food from the cafeteria. I've already missed my first class, so I'll go to Mortal Combat at noon. Mortal Combat is similar to gym class. It's a physical class where you learn to defeat your opponent instead of doing jumping jacks. I have to get physically and mentally prepared if I plan to battle Prince again. Besides, the teacher doesn't tolerate any slacking.

Opening the door, I grimace and feel a faint

tingle in my chest. I'm not sure if I'm anxious about entering or afraid that someone will attack me again. I replay the event in my head. They had done a good job at cleaning the blood. Only a faint brown stain is left on the carpet. Still, I can't figure out how he escaped with no one seeing him. The headmaster had to see him racing from the room, holding his balls.

My gaze trails the carpet to Grace's desk, broken into several pieces. She must be angry because we broke her desk during the fight. But hell, I was fighting for my life.

After I iron my uniform and get dressed, I head down to the cafeteria. Approaching the cafeteria makes me get a sinking sensation in my chest. I always got weird stares. Now the stares are death stares. Students I've never met walk past me, frowning for no good reason. I'm sure I've done nothing to these strangers.

I hold my head up and continue walking to the grille area, even though I feel like a cast member on survivor and I'm on the island alone.

After I get a burrito, I locate Grace sitting at a table with two girls. I scurry over to the table. At least there is someone here who will speak to me.

I slide my tray on the table and set my backpack

on the floor. The two girls that Grace was talking to give me a dirty sneer. "Is this your roommate?" one girl says, her oversized lips popping. She pushes a few strands of her green hair behind her ear. She has tattoos galore. There's even one in the center of her neck: an eyeball. Don't know what that means. Stupid tattoo, if you ask me. The other girl with blonde hair, named Journey, is the ringleader.

She and her friends are the mean girl crew. I don't know why Grace would associate herself with them. I won't give her the satisfaction to assume she intimidates me. Because she doesn't. I'll whip her ass here in this cafeteria and won't think twice about it.

Grace flips a glance my way. "Yeah, she's my roommate," she says in a low tone. It seems as if she is ashamed to say I'm her roommate.

She doesn't give me a warm welcome home, doesn't ask 'How was the awful night you spent on a hard, cold, steel-ass bench?' Instead, she gives me a glare as if she assumes I'm guilty. It's the same glare the headmaster and that thick-ass officer gave me. I expected more from Grace. I don't give two fucks about what the mean girls think. Grace is better than that.

Blonde barbie and her flunky stand and excuse themselves from the table. I'm delighted. I didn't come here to see those bitches, anyway. I'm more concern that Grace is giving me the cold shoulder.

"Grace, please get your frustration off your chest," I grunt.

Her face turns an apple red. She sighs, but she knows I'm serious. "Ronnie, I have a ton of questions. This isn't the appropriate place."

"You realize I was fighting for my life?" Squaring my shoulders, I move back. I need to see her face. Her facial expression would help me gauge her feelings.

Small frown lines cross her face as she speaks. "Everyone is saying that Kenny killed your friend Shelly," she barks.

"You know that's not true."

Her disbelief quickly fills the cramped space. It's apparent that she doesn't believe me. My heart hammers in my chest as I realize she isn't my friend either.

"The rumors are that you helped. Now you're trying to frame Prince." Her eyes bulge as she awaits a response.

I jerk my head back and stall for a second. "What, are you crazy? You can't believe that. Prince killed Shelly and several other girls. Is anybody saying that?" I growl in a sassy, witch sort of way. My body temperature is skyrocketing with anger.

"So, what happened in the room?" Her stare pierces through my face. "It's a mess. My desk is broken and there was blood everywhere." She rests her chin on her palm.

"Prince attacked me in the room."

"No one saw him. The rumor is that the head-master had you arrested after he witnessed a pool of blood."

Now my voice is elevated. "I was bleeding. I'm out of jail. They had the wrong person." I suppress an eye-roll, tapping my hand on my lap.

I'm sick and tired of all the rumors. Either she is with me or she ain't. But I'm not going to keep explaining shit to anybody.

"I don't know. This is enormous. Too much to digest." She throws her hands up. "Everyone on campus dislikes you right now. Prince has many friends here. He can make your life a living hell. I only have a few more semesters. I don't need to be associated with this shit," she hisses.

"What are you saying?"

"I'm saying I requested a new roommate."

"Grace, I have no other friends here."

I hoped Grace would always be in my corner. But

at the first sign of danger, she hops ship. What kind of friend is she? She only cares about herself.

"Grace, if someone hurt you, I would risk my life trying to find justice for you."

"No matter what you do, it will not bring Shelly back. She's gone." She shrugs as if Shelly was an old piece of furniture.

"I know that. But I will sleep a lot easier knowing the right person is in prison for her murder."

"Be honest with yourself. Are you doing this because the killer is loose? Or is it out of guilt?"

"Guilt for what?" I squint.

"Because she was there with you." She wagged her finger in my face. "You got so drunk that you don't remember what happened. Or you want Kenny out of jail? Even though you are uncertain that Kenny did it. You were sloppy drunk, remember?"

I feel two feet tall, as if Mother scorned me for stealing candy. She stands from the table and grabs her tray. "I'll catch you later."

I grind my teeth. I'm so angry I could have slapped the shit out of Grace. How could she question me? I was drunk and I feel guilty enough without her rubbing it in my face.

Was she being a friend, trying to give me a reality check? I'm going crazy wracking my brains for every little detail of that night. I get snippets here and there. One person stands out: Prince. I'm sure Shelly was talking with him that night. That doesn't prove murder, but the nightmares I have tell me the truth. It was Prince, and no one can change my mind.

I snatch my backpack from the floor, leaving my tray on the table. I've lost my fucking appetite.

Sighing, I think about my next class. I despise Mortal Combat class; it's physically draining. But I must pass or else they will ship me back home. I'm not sure which one is worse: the slum I grew up in or being framed for a crime I didn't commit.

Sweat clings to the nape of my neck as I change into my gym clothes: burgundy shorts and a grey t-shirt with Ash Academy written across the front. The uniform is cringe-worthy, but it's clean. I've learned to appreciate everyone wearing the same clothes. No one will tease me about my rags.

The locker room is filled with a bunch of half-naked females, some showering, others get changed for class. Whispering catches my attention. I turn my gaze and see Jennifer and Whitney. Their sneaky stares my way tells me I'm the topic of chatter. Staring at them, I don't blink, letting them know I'm onto them.

If they have shit to say, there's no point in whispering. Whitney shouldn't gossip about anyone. Everyone has been gossiping about her hair, saying it's a weave. She lies and tells everyone it's her natural hair.

The fire burns within me and I can no longer hold my tongue. All day, filthy stares have taunted me. "You have something to say?" I question as my flaming gaze trails them from head to toe.

Jennifer snickers, covering her mouth, trying to hide her crooked teeth.

"Nothing to say to you," Whitney says in a low growl.

I slam my locker in anger, wiping the smile from Jennifer's face. I storm out to the gym floor. I remind myself that I don't need any more trouble.

The teacher, Mr. Moore, comes out with shorts pulled up past his belly button and socks that reach his knees. I don't know why he dresses so weirdly. He has never seen a mirror, I suppose.

He instructs us on exercises. We begin our warm-up before drills. Although I'm extremely fatigued, I participate. It helps force last night out of my head. The situation only makes me angry.

Meanwhile, the twins' faces keep popping into my head. I love Kenny, but for some unknown reason, I keep lusting over both of the twins.

Mr. Moore blows his whistle. I let out a huff. Finally, we are done with these exercises.

"I will pair you each up with an opponent. Ladies, it is mind over matter," Mr. Moore exclaims. He walks back to the bleachers and takes a seat. He is not more in shape than a couch potato. "You should control the battle with your hands and mind. Save the magic for an actual battle."

Sluggishly, I strut over to the rack and grab my boxing gloves. Again, the whispering sounds behind me. This time I hear my name.

I pivot around and my gaze lands on Jennifer and Whitney. The bitches are going too far. I put my hand to my ear. "Did you say something?"

"We know you helped Kenny kill your friend. "

"You don't know shit. Stop running your mouth while your ahead."

"Why do you have such an attitude with us? We're just reporting what everyone on campus is saying," Whitney says as she throws her hand on her hip.

"I don't want your fucking reports. Leave me alone," I warn.

"Jennifer and Ronielle to the center mat, please." Mr. Moore yells.

She better shut the fuck up before we make it to the mat or her ass is grass and I'm the lawn mower.

"Damn, he wants me to battle the evil killer," Jennifer mumbles.

I let out a sigh, trying to stay calm. My temperature is rising uncontrollably. The rage has caused my hands to ball into fists. I stare down at my hands. I realize my fists are so tight, my knuckles have turned white. Mr. Moore said its mind over matter. Jennifer's words are dancing all over my mind. I'm ready to unleash the beast that is sizzling at the surface of my skin.

One more word from her is going to send me over the edge. Then I'm whipping her ass.

We stand on the mat as Mr. Moore blows the whistle. Wearing big boxing gloves is a disadvantage for me. I prefer to use my bare hands. She throws the first jab then sweeps her hand across her body as if she taunting me. She got the first jab, but she won't get the last.

Looking at her ugly face makes me more enraged. A grin crisscrosses her face. She started it, and I'm going to finish it. She flicks a glance at Whitney. Whitney nods in approval. She thinks I'm scared. She has the wrong fucking woman. I raise my hand, then stare my enemy in the eye and swing a punch, landing right on her face.

My head is telling me that it's a good one. That was my way of letting her know not to fuck with me. My anger is over brewing as I step back. She takes another quick swing, missing my face by an inch. She was so close I felt the wind from her swift jab.

Her face turns an angry red as we circle each other around the mat.

"You think you're tough shit," she yells before taking another swing.

This time I duck. I realize I'm letting my anger get the best of me. I take a heady breath as my heartrate lowers. Narrowing my gaze at my target's face, I drive my fist back. My punch lands on her left eye.

"You bitch," she screams while unlacing her boxing gloves.

So I unlace my boxing gloves. This bitch won't get the best of me. Steam floats from her face as she charges toward me.

I brace myself for the fight that's coming. But my vision has become red. Everything else has faded out, but voices wail in the background. "I told she is a killer," a feminine voice claims. I'm not a killer, but my killer instinct has kicked in.

My head is yanked forward as she pulls my hair. I swing several punches toward her face, one after another.

I'm sick of all her taunting comments. This will teach the bitches to leave me alone. I'm a savage. I came from the inner city where I had to be tough or I wouldn't have survived. I've fought bitches twice as big as her frail ass.

A sharp pain penetrates my face. I think this girl just scratched me. My punches become even stronger. Suddenly I'm yanked away. I continue swinging, even though some has separated us. I hit nothing but air.

"Calm down, ladies," Mr. Moore screams.

"She started it," I yell, starting at her face. She is bleeding with a swollen left eye. Her hair is in disarray. It looks like she had a fight with a lion.

"See, I told you she's crazy," Whitney yells. "She was trying to kill her like she did her friend."

I charge toward her. Mr. Jones, the other mortal combat teacher, tightens his grip around my wrist.

"Whitney, that is enough. Have a seat on the bench," Mr. Moore requests.

Mr. Jones halls me back to the locker room as Jennifer yells, "This isn't over!"

She's right: it sure as hell isn't. With as angry as I am, next time I see her, she's going to have a problem.

"Calm down," Mr. Jones says.

I try to calm down, but my adrenaline is racing. I continue trying to escape his captivity.

"I will let you go once you are calm," he says in a low tone.

"Okay."

"What's going on with you?" he says. He releases his grip around my wrist.

"She started it!" I scream at the top of my lungs.

"I'm standing right next to you. There's no need to yell." He towers over me. He's six feet six inches tall, at least. He's a wolf shifter, but he doesn't have that growl, that killer instinct.

He was right, I didn't mean to yell at Mr. Jones. He is nothing but nice to me. My face drops as tears stream down my face.

"It's okay," he says.

"No, they keep messing with me. I'm not a murderer. I didn't kill anyone."

"I know, Ronielle," he says as the locker room door squeaks as it's opened.

"Ronielle, go to detention."

"Me?" I scream, turning my attention to Mr. Moore. "Why?"

"Because you threw the first punch and she is bleeding everywhere." He points to the door.

"Didn't you year what she said to me?"

"No, I didn't hear Jennifer say anything. Besides, those are words."

"But they hurt."

"I'm sure they do. You better hope she doesn't press charges."

Fine, I'll go. I need to get out of this gym before I beat Whitney's ass next.

6

I tossed and turned all night, knowing today I'd have to serve detention. They had the nerve to give me three detentions, for shit I didn't start. It's like a prison in there. But it's even worse, because you can't talk to anyone. You need an interesting book or time stops. Sitting, staring at a clock all day is not productive for me. I could be out canvassing the neighborhood, searching for the serial killer.

I didn't hear the alarm, but my eyes slam open, leaving my gaze on the ceiling. "When is my life going to change?" I huff. There's a wonderful life waiting for me. I must get through the destruction first.

My alarm sounds and I hit the snooze button.

Force of habit, I guess. I don't need any more sleep; I'm already wide awake. I flip a glance over at Grace's bed, which is empty.

I don't know if she went over to her boyfriend's house to visit or to avoid me. She says she's requesting a transfer and since Ash is overcrowded this semester, good luck with finding a new room. Some kind of friend she is. A frown twists at my lips as I think about her.

I force myself up and glare at the overflowing pile of clothes in my laundry basket. I haven't had time for laundry. Or anything else. I've been so consumed with finding the killer. But I must make laundry a priority this weekend or I'll be wearing my panties inside out.

Heading for the bathroom, I grab a face towel, the one thing I have clean. I take a hot shower, trying to scrub the horrific last couple of weeks from my mind. It doesn't matter how hard I try, I can't stop the vision of her face. I find myself daydreaming. How different would my life be if Shelly was alive?

I wish I could talk to her one last time. I'd tell her how terribly sorry I am. It's true, I left her alone. What a terrible friend I've been.

I hop out the shower and get dressed. A click from the doorknob brings a sharp pain to my gut. I grab a pair of curling irons from the cabinet. Whoever is here is getting their ass beat. Holding my breath, I try to be silent as I ease toward the door.

I crack it open and peek out, not seeing anything in view. I open the door more, then step into the bedroom with the curlers gripped tightly in my hands.

My gaze lands on Grace's blue eyes. I let a long sigh escape my lips. My heart still hammers in my chest. I was scared to death. Everyone hates me; it could have been any student searching for revenge.

She flicks me a frown, eyebrows furrowing. Swiftly, she turns her head. As if she slept here last night. She is such a fucking follower. She has no brain of her own. Following the crowd in hating me is pathetic. She could at least speak. Rolling my eyes, I try hiding my disapproval by focusing on my backpack.

"Good morning to you too," I say sarcastically. I grab my book bag from my desk. The tension is too thick for me.

She still says nothing. She continues unpacking her book bag. I don't know how we can coexist, especially until next semester.

She has a total attitude toward me. When she is

here, I'll try avoiding her. She will apologize when she realizes she's been wrong this entire time.

I storm out the room, slamming the door behind me. I have detention to serve.

SINCE I'M CURSED with the worst luck, I should've assumed it was coming.

They put me in detention with the mean girls. Three of them: Taniesha, Kelly, and Paige. They all attend Mage Academy. I'm sure they are in here for violating the dress code. There skirts are always tight and short. They get them a size too small. And they cut their shirts, turning them into belly tops, exposing their pierced belly buttons.

Also, there are the rough looking males: wizards and mages. Scowls and frowns galore trail me from head to toe. I don't know why we share detention hall with Mage and Supernatural Academies.

Fuck.

I enter the room, clinging onto my back as if it's a precious weapon. No one speaks, but the stares continue. I imagine what they're thinking. I can almost read their thoughts. Here comes the killer.

The teacher sits at her desk, nearly asleep with

her coffee mug sitting at the table. I assume there are no assigned seats. I take the first one available nearest to the door in case I need to escape.

"And you are?" Ms. Finn, the less-than-nice teacher questions.

"Ronielle Simms," I respond.

She looks up at me, eyes bulging and her lips parting. "Ms. Simms, how nice of you to join us," she says sternly, frowning.

I glance at the clock. I'm only two minutes late.

Jennifer comes walking in the door. Switching like she modeling. She has on sunglasses to cover that shiner she has. The teacher stays quiet. She doesn't grill her about her name.

Jennifer takes a seat as far from me as she can get. Which is a good idea. If she starts some shit today, there will be a brawl in detention. I take a hard swallow.

"Students, please finish your homework. I'm sure you have plenty to do," Ms. Finn barks.

Funny thing is, she didn't say anything to Jennifer, and she strolled in later than me and wearing sunglasses. The teachers here all conspire to destroy me.

I'm sure there's a huge rumor amongst the staff as well. The headmaster went to my room only to find a room filled with blood. I don't know what he thinks but I didn't beat my own ass. And I didn't hurt anyone else.

The three mean girls in the back whisper, probably about me. Not today. I won't fall into the trap. As long as they don't say it to my face.

"Jennifer, come sit by us," Kelly says, flicking her artificial nails. My nostrils flare as a frown twists upon my lips.

Jennifer gathers her things, quickly racing over and taking a seat next to the pack. She rarely runs in that circle, but I suppose they have something in common. They all hate me.

"Pssst," someone from the hall hisses. I dart my gaze toward the door. All I see is the bare white hall walls and the cream-colored shiny tall.

I turn my attention back to my potions and spells book, searching for a potion that could get rid of Jennifer.

"Pssst." The sound wafts from the hall again. This time I view a shadow from my peripheral. I peer my gaze up from my book and my heartrate triples in speed at the faces in the hall.

7

*A* smirk nips at my lips. My stare is fixed on Josh and James standing in the hall, in the flesh, looking like twin movie stars. How did they get out of jail? I'm sure Kenny helped them; he said he would try.

"Ms. Ronielle, back to your studies," Ms. Finn scolds. She rises from her desk, staring me square in the eye. Pure evil dances across her face. She drives her feet in the floor as if she is angry. Scowling at the twins, she slams the door in their faces, but not before I hold up one finger, telling them to wait for me. Detention period is almost over, although I have two more periods to serve.

"This is not social hour," she growls while

standing in front of my desk. She looks like an angry bird. She said nothing to the mean girls, who are in the back cackling. A groan escapes my lips, then I lower my gaze to my book, ignoring her. Her scent of caramel flavored coffee tickles my stomach. She wears stockings the same color as the coffee she drinks.

I feel a sense of relieved pressure. The twins' freedom means I have two friends. We have something in common: they want Prince and so do I.

After ten long minutes, the bell sounds. The entire class races toward the door like a stampede. "Ronielle, I need to speak with you," Ms. Finn says.

"Sorry, I have to get my next class," I respond as I walk out of the classroom. She must be insane if she thinks I'm going to spend an extra second in detention. She had an hour to talk to me and she didn't.

Searching for the twins, my eyes scour the hall. I spot the twins waiting near the cafeteria. My vagina twitches at the site of them. I nearly jump into their arms. "How did you guys get out? I'm so happy you are here." My heart does a funny pitter patter thing. I'm not sure what it means, but every time I'm in the presence of the twins, my heart goes wild. Neurons fire in places unspeakable.

It really doesn't matter how they got out. I'm delighted to see them.

By the flirting in Josh's sexy wink, he's happy to see me too. We walk down the hall and I feel more secure having two big men beside me. Though it doesn't stop the other students from giving me devilish stares.

"We need to ask you something important, but we'll wait until we get out into the courtyard," James suggests.

A female student struts toward us, her hair flowing and her dingy shirt tight on her oversized breasts. At first glance, I get defensive. From afar, it appears she's frowning at me. The closer we get to her, the more I realize she isn't grinning. She's nearly drooling, staring at the twins. That's enough to piss me off. *Stay away, they're mine.*

She is a pretty girl. I don't know much about her, except that she is always flirting. The twins must be accustomed to females throwing themselves at them. I don't know how I hadn't seen them on campus before.

"Hello, twins." She frowns and her eyes widen at the sight of me. "What are you guys doing with this killer?" She darts her gaze at me, then rolls her eyes. She raises her less-than-perfect eyebrows, waiting for me to respond. Like I'm going to deny it. I'm sick of explaining myself to everyone on this campus. I don't owe them shit.

James holds his hand up in her face. "Wait, hold up. You don't know her. Leave her alone."

"I know she's a killer. it's all over campus. She's a snake who killed her own friend." She wags her finger inches away from my face. I take two steps back, maintaining my composure. I imagine myself punching her in the face. Silently I'm screaming, but I'm able to control my rage. I don't want to add any more time to that already hefty sentence of detention.

"We're not going to let you bash her. Keep it moving," James says, grabbing me by my hand. He leads me out the door with Josh following.

I flip a glance over my back. She is standing there gasping for air. She likes the twins in more than a friendly way, but neither of them are interested.

Grateful the twins have my back, I breathe a sigh of relief. They have gained my trust. In my eyes, they are even sexier.

The sun kisses my skin as I walk out the door. I blink and cover my eyes from the brightness. The sky has been dark and dingy for weeks. I've forgotten how comforting the sun is. It soothes my cool face.

James finds an empty bench and takes a seat. Josh and I follow his lead.

"So, what did you guys bring me out here for?" I question as I stare at the grass. I'm viewing the campus from a new lens. The sun brightens everything around us. Similar to my happiness, this too is temporary.

"We need a favor," James says. I realize it's James because when he smiles, he has dimples. Josh doesn't have dimples.

"Sure, whatever you need." I flick a gaze at them both.

Josh pauses and gives me a blank stare. He doesn't want to ask. Then I get curious. It better not be something ridiculous. I have enough stress in my life. The loud alarm sounds in the back of my mind, my internal radar alerting me of bullshit.

"No, it's nothing crazy," James says. He views my expression, my resting bitch face.

"We want you to go public with us. Tell everybody that Prince is the killer. And we will say we think he has our sister."

A bolt of hot magic clogs my throat. I promised Kenny I'd stay away from this case. Not that I wouldn't keep investigating, but that I'd keep my silence.

"What do you mean, go public?" I question.

"Call the news reporter. Put it all on blast," James explains.

I cringe, shaking my head. "No. I can't do that," I respond.

"Why not?" James growls.

"Everyone already hates me."

"This way could clear your name," Josh says.

"But it won't. We don't have proof. They will still blame me." I shudder closer to them. "Everyone will hate the two of you."

"We're okay with that. As long as we get our sister back," James urges.

I lean back on the bench and ponder about what they're asking. If I go through with this, I will lose Kenny's trust, but at least Prince won't be able to walk the streets. And I won't get all the dirty stares and the aggressive comments.

I give them an apprehensive look. "Okay, I'll do it."

"Thank you," James yells before planting a kiss on my lips. Initially, I jerk back in shock. He comes closer and continues kissing me. Who am I to stop him? I kiss him for a few seconds. From the way his tongue is dancing across my mouth, the sex will be magical.

I pull away. "What was that for?"

"I'm sorry. I was just happy." He shrugs.

Operation Take Prince Down is a go.

8

---

*I* take the dreaded hike over to the police station. Although it's only a few city blocks, the cold Chicago wind makes it seems a lot further. The frigid weather nips at my fingertips, so I shove my hands into my pocket.

Going public with my accusation of Prince is as chilling as the weather. Nightmares jolted me awake in a cold sweat last night. I'm scared shitless to tell the entire city, but someone has to speak for Shelly and the twin's sister. If not me, then who?

Today I'm requesting to see Kenny. If he's going to hear about the news, I should be the one to inform him. He will be pissed, considering I lied to him. But he must understand this is about putting the true criminal in prison. It's beneficial to everyone: Kenny, the twins, and me.

I enter the police station. It's the last place I want to be again. But at least this time I'm not cuffed. The same rude, tall-ass male guard is at the counter. The one who arrested me. He doesn't talk much, so I don't know why he's working the front desk.

"Excuse me." I tap my hand on the desk. "I want to put in a request to visit an inmate," I bark.

The officer doesn't move. He continues writing as if he didn't even hear me.

Clearing my throat, I tap the desk a second time. He keeps jotting something down. I guess I'll wait until he's done. He has some serious character flaws and lack of social skills. An officer is probably not the job for him. He needs a job where he doesn't deal with the public.

He straightens his tie and then flicks me a nonchalant look. "How can I help you?"

I cringe, suppressing an eye roll. "Can I schedule a visit with an inmate?" I growl.

"Sure," he says as he grabs a large black book from underneath the cabinet.

Don't they have a computer system for visits? I see computers on several of the desks. I bet he can't navigate the computer system. He responds slower than most. Even his speech is slower.

"Who do you want to visit?"

"Kenneth."

He flips through a few pages then grabs his mug with steam dancing around the rim. He takes a sip of the warm drink slowly. As if I have all day. *Hurry the fuck up, I've got a class soon.* "Oh yes, here he is. You can visit him on Thursday," he suggests.

"Thursday?" I question. "But today is Tuesday."

"That's right," he says. "He has a visit today and tomorrow." He closes the book. "You can see him on Thursday."

I slam my hand on the desk, rattling his mug. His beady eyes meet my gaze. Without saying a word, his face says "It's time for you to go."

I storm out of the station before curse words float from my mouth like smoke and I get arrested. I want to visit Kenny, but I don't want to share a cell with him.

Who is visiting Kenneth today and tomorrow? It better not be another witch.

I HURRY to my next class, which is on Mage's campus. If I want to graduate on time, I must take a course on their campus. Magical elements 101. It's quite an interesting class. We are at the beginning stages of how to use magic. This week we are supposed to learn to ride brooms. Everyone, even the mages. I'm really looking forward to today's class.

Scrambling through the back door of class, I wipe the sweat from my brow. The sound of the bell pierces my ears. Barely made it in time. Professor Harvey is writing some jibberish on the board. He writes most of the time, since most of the class can barely make out what he says.

I flip my book out awaiting our assignment. My gaze narrows in on the writing on the board. My heart stalls, small knots weaving in the out of my stomach.

We need a partner. No student will partner with me. I'm the black sheep. Anyway, why do we need to partner with someone just to learn to ride a broom?

"Everyone get a partner," Mr. Harvey says. Everyone scatters and begins to chit-chat with their friends. All the students find someone except me and another witch, April.

"Ok, Ronielle and April, pair up." He slips his

jacket on and grabs a book from his desk. "We are going outside today for our lesson on broom riding."

April's eyes flicker and she frowns. "No, I'm mot partnering with her," she grunts.

The heifer has a problem. I don't want to partner with her either. I can work alone; I'm an introvert, anyway.

The door knob twists, silencing the room. I'm grateful another brawl is brewing. The twins enter the room and I nearly faint. They always show up right on time. How did they know I'm on the edge of trouble?

They walk over to Mr. Harvey's desk. I can't take my eyes off them. It's a miracle they got this class.

James shows Mr. Harvey his schedule. They both take a seat up front. Josh winks at me before he sits. Passion sizzles in my chest.

"Okay class, we have two guys joining the class. James and Josh McFarland." He points at the twins. He coughs, covering his mouth. "Now, where were we? Oh yes, find a partner for the assignment today."

April gives me the stank face. She gets up and struts toward James. "He can be my partner," she says.

"Fine. Then the other twin…what's your name?"

Josh stalls for a minute. I guess he hasn't learned Mr. Harvey's accent. "Josh."

"Yes. Josh, you will partner with Ronielle here."

"No problem," he says before smiling at me.

"Okay everyone, grab a broom from the closet."

I slip on my coat then zip up. I stroll over to Josh's desk. His gaze trails my physique from head to toe. He holds the broom in his hand

"Let's go, shall we?" he says then we walk to the door. "You know how to ride, don't you?" he whispers.

I bat my eyelashes. "Of course."

9

We step onto the football field as the golden sun is fading from view. The sun hides behind the clouds, much like I want to hide. Suddenly I'm nervous as hell for this riding session. I have never ridden a broom, never even tried before. Not to mention I'm clumsy and my balance is off. But to pass this class, I'm going to give it a go. Besides, I know Josh won't let anything happen to me. Amusing, honestly: a witch afraid to ride a broom.

I flip a glance over at James and April. She is getting way to comfortable with James. I find myself jealous. I have a boyfriend, but I'm protective of the twins. April is an evil witch who won't get her claws into James. Not if I have something to say about it.

Josh lays the broom flat on the field and stares at me.

"What?" I question as my pale lips curl into a smile. Flirting, I blink my long lashes.

"You must summon the broom to rise. At least to here." He grabs my waist. "That will make it easier for you to hop on."

Biting my bottom lip, I give him a blank stare then shift my gaze around the football field. The other students have at least gotten their broom off the ground.

"Have you ever ridden before?" Josh asks.

I shake my head no. It's quite pathetic. A witch who has never ridden a broom. But Mother never taught me.

He giggles. "Where do you live? Under a rock?"

"This is a 101 class. He should teach me," I grunt.

"Yes, but you know the basics." His eyes bulge. "How to get it off the ground. Don't worry, I'll show you," he assures me.

He flips a quick stare at the broom. His face reddens with no movement. I guess he is concentrating. I'm thinking about how handsome he looks when he's serious.

Within a few seconds, the broom rises from the ground, stopping at my waist.

"Oh, magnificent job," I yell. The broom swiftly plummets to the ground.

"The key is mind over matter," he says

I have to concentrate and quit letting my lustful emotions take over. "I get it. I have to clear my head, let my magic float through me."

"That's right." He grabs his hat from his pocket and slips it on his head.

If I could channel this angry energy, I'd get this broom flying in no time. My magic would shatter across the entire football field.

A faint thrum of magic buzzes through my veins. It never works. A magical dud is what I am. I never had to use it before. I'm always in a crisis that takes over my thoughts. Concentration is what I need.

"If supernaturals are distracting, close your eyes," he whispers.

Grinding my teeth, I keep my eyes shut. My mind goes blank, except for the thought of the broom.

The chatter of my classmates wails in the background.

"You're doing a good job," Josh says softly.

I slightly open my eyes to see the broom at my side. I'm overwhelmed with joy. I can't believe I got the broom to move.

"Stay focused," Josh says. "As long as you concentrate on the broom, it won't fall."

I concentrate hard on the broom. I want to get a good grade. I want to ride. I'd prefer James be the driver and I ride on back, but we don't get graded that way. Everyone has to show they can ride.

"Ok, you got it to your waist. Now hop on."

I hesitate. I can see myself flying straight into a tree, making a fool out of myself in front of the entire class. That would give them more ammunition to talk behind my back.

Slowly, I raise my leg then flick it over the broom. Shaking, the broom rumbles underneath me. This broom better stay still, or I'm going to fall flat on my ass.

I position myself on the stick and take in a heady breath of pollution. My feet are planted on the ground. The broom jerks and I firmly grab ahold of the stick.

James snickers. "You're not skilled enough to ride without hands."

My grip becomes a little tighter as the broom jerks once more.

"Keep both your hands on the stick," Josh urges. "Guide the broom in the direction you choose."

"Ok, I got it."

I move my hands forward and take my feet off the ground. The broom jolts forward, sucking the wind from my chest. I drop my feet to the ground. The movement fascinated me.

I'm extremely proud that I had the courage to attempt a spin on a broom. I've heard about broom rides. Mother had ridden in the past. She described it as a euphoric feeling. She said once you ride, it's addicting.

I lift my legs once more and the broom escalates up. Before I know it, I'm ten feet off the ground.

Mr. Harvey yells, "Good job!" But I didn't take my mind off riding this broom. I escalate a few more feet than I move forward, gliding through the air like a kite. My hair flows back. A smile forces its way on my lips. The wind rushes across my face. I want to lift my hands in the air and soar. The air smells better. My mind is clear. My heart rate is low. The noise has vanished; it's just me and space. No worries of time or slanderous gossip. Liberating is how I describe the sensation. I drop years of stress and dead weight to the ground. Suddenly, I'm as light as a feather.

Mother was right. Gliding through this air is like, I imagine, drug intoxication. I swivel to the left, dodging a building. Should I fly away and never return? Forget all the chaos in my life? I consider it for a split second. I soon realize I have too many obligations. I owe Shelly and Kenny.

I continue riding as if I have a destination. Finally, I swivel around and head back toward the football field.

I descend, and I see the twinkle in James's eyes even from ten feet in the air. His eyes spin with desire. I hope I'm not giving James the wrong impression. Well, I can't be. It's true. I want them both.

Why do I have to choose? Guys never do.

The grim feeling and the elevated heart rate return. Seeing the other students and their distasteful looks brings back painful negativity.

I come to a halt above Josh's head, and I slowly descend to the ground.

"That was the most liberating experience ever," I boast.

"Once you learn to channel the rest of your magic, Ms. Simms, you will be an exceptional witch," Mr. Harvey says.

10

I sit amongst the misfits in my last detention. I only had three periods, but it felt like an eternity. Humid, musty, and loud: that describes the student body today. It's annoying that no one will talk with me. Guess I should get accustomed to not having any female friends. Fuck them. I don't need them to survive.

Huffing, I rearrange myself on the hard, uncomfortable wooden seats. If this is their tactic to keep us paying attention to the lesson, they failed. Detention is horrible. It's almost as bad as prison. I will consider that the next time one of these witches starts a brawl.

I'm never fighting again. Well, I won't say never. But I'm going to control my temper. Kenny says I shouldn't let anyone get the best of me. He's right. I'm going to mind my own affairs and shut my big mouth.

I lower my gaze back to my book as a trickle of sweat rolls down my back. The piercing stares of the misfits burns the nape of my neck. Their constant snickers and giggles irritates me. It's borderline harassment, but no one at this school will support me. Everything is my fault since I'm considered an accessory to a murder. Ms. Robinson says nothing. She lets them continue their chatter. They run Mage Academy. The teachers are even afraid of them.

They're gossiping about me. As long as they continue to whisper, I'm cool. If one of them touches me, it will be a different story.

The sweltering heat has me wet in private places. I'm uncomfortable in here. I raise my hand.

"Yes?" Ms. Robinson asks, her green eyes stuck to my face.

"Ms. Robinson, can you turn the heat down?" The heat is extreme. I could swear the devil is sitting behind me.

She lowers her glasses. "I have no control of the heat. Remove your sweater, dear."

Ms. Robinson is a cool teacher, better than the last teacher. Every day it's a new instructor. No one wants this job. We are supposed to read or do another mundane task. The teachers sit at the desk reading current events, allowing some students autonomy while the rest of us have to sit quietly.

I remind myself constantly that I didn't come here to fight or waste time in detention. My goal is to learn magic. I've learned how to ride a broom. That's progress, but not much.

I swivel my sweater off, but I need to get out of this class.

A faint tap on my shoulder from behind startles me. I don't pay it any attention. The giggles from behind me echo in my head. I'm sure it's one of the asshole misfits.

"Psssst," a feminine voice hisses from behind. The old Ronnie wants to turn around and scream. The new Ronnie keeps silent. I'm proud that I can maintain my composure. A piece of paper floats over my shoulder, landing on my desk.

I'm hesitant to touch it. The supernaturals hate me. This note could kick my rage into top gear. But curiosity gets the best of me. I pry the note open.

**We know what you did, killer. Watch your back.**

That's all they've got? To get me upset enough to

fight, someone has to slap me. Though I can't say I'm not irritated.

Already my eye is twitching in anger. I flip a gaze over my shoulder. I view the silly smirks on all three of their faces. Wanting to slap the grins off their faces, I quickly twist around.

I reach for my bookmark that lays next to my water bottle. I save the spot in my elemental magic guide and close the book. I can feel a storm of emotions. My witch attitude is brewing. Without raising my hand, I ask, "Ms. Robinson, can I go to the ladies room?" Before I knock one of these blondes out of the chair.

"Go ahead," she hisses as if she wanted to say no. It doesn't matter if she did. I was going to march out of the class, anyway. You can't prevent someone from going to the bathroom. Unless she wants me to urinate right here.

Quietly, I scurry out the classroom. I don't need to use the ladies' room, but I must escape this classroom.

Barging into the bathroom, a sigh squeaks from my lips. I hurry to the faucet and fling cold water on my face. I don't care that it will destroy my makeup. I just need to calm down. Those girls know it pisses me off. That's why they keep attacking me.

I remind myself that it's Wednesday. Tomorrow I can visit Kenny. A sense of peace washes over me. My heart rate rages and a ball of emotions descends.

I better get back to class before Ms. Robinson comes searching for me. I hurry out of the bathroom and notice Grace a few feet away. I want to speak to her. This awkward anger toward each other is frivolous. I miss her. But for me to express my emotions to her would require me to trust her. Maybe I will make the first step in mending our friendship.

But the scowl crossing her face is pure hatred. I don't know what I did to her in particular. I will not beg her to be my friend. Or kiss her ass. She rolls her eyes at the sight of me and continues down the hall with her friends as if she never met me.

It's killing me inside, but I won't dare let her see it bothers me.

As I get closer to detention, I hear whispers. They are trying to whisper, but the conversation is clear. Although I can't see faces, it's the headmaster and Ms. Robinson talking. No one is usually in the halls during class times.

Tip toeing, I inch closer, careful not to make a sound.

"I don't know why Prince is on a spree," the headmaster says.

"What is he looking for? This is horrendous for our school system," Ms. Robinson says in a panic.

"He's weak," the headmaster says.

I sneak into class, terrified of what I just witnessed.

Prince is dangerous and everyone on this campus knows. Why is there a big cover up? The headmaster said he never heard of Prince.

11

My inner self is ranting this morning. Why is life so cruel to me? I dread waking up. Usually, sleep is the most peace I have. I'm not a morning person. I remind myself that today I'm going to visit Kenny. Immediately, my somber mood turns into in a flood of endorphins. I hop up in bed and toss the cover aside. Putting my feet on the floor in search of my slippers, I giggle when I don't find them. Normally I would get irritated, but nothing is bringing down my mood.

Excited, I flick on the television to watch the morning news. As I ramble through my dresser for clothes, I overhear the reporter. I twist around and sheer horror penetrates my soul. My body physically jerks as I stare at the television.

Another girl from Mage Academy has gone missing. The prestigious Academy and its sister campuses have had several girls go missing. Two in this month alone.

I cover my mouth. Oh, shit, Prince has struck again. Now everyone on campus will know it wasn't Kenny or me. A surge of doubt invades my head. Knowing this school, they might say I acted alone. Everyone on this campus knows the truth, yet no one will say anything. It is unnerving.

Today I'm demanding Kenny's freedom. They must release him now. I'll tell him I'm going public with the twins, calling Prince out on his bullshit.

Trembling, I finish watching the news in complete disbelief. He almost got away with murder. There's a mountain of evidence against him now. Shelly isn't his first murder. I'm certain it won't be the last. Unless he's stopped. How stupid can one criminal be?

I grab my jacket from the closet before heading to the campus police station. Half of Grace's clothes have vanished. I guess she moved them out piece by piece when I wasn't here. Now she needs to apologize. Not that it matters. She judged me and followed the crowd in this witch hunt. Some friend she is.

Racing out door, I grab my keys and book bag. I can't wait to tell Kenny. I'm sure they hear the news at the police station. And to think Monday he's scheduled to be transported to a jail.

As I open the police station door, a foul scent of urine consumes the air. I can smell even with my stunted senses. I'm so excited even a funky scent won't run me off.

"Hello, I'm here to see Kenneth Strong," I say proudly. The female officer that questioned me before sits at the front desk. She has on a different wig. It's still hideous. Better than the last wig, though. We exchange scowls, then she shifts her gaze back to the computer.

"What's your name?" she questions. She knows good and well what my name is. They don't get many prisoners. Especially females. She remembers me.

"Ronielle Simms."

She hunts and pecks at the keyboard. She lifts her head and rises from the chair. She struts toward the front counter, taking her time. "Here. Write your name down," she says, handing me a clipboard.

A scribble down my name and slide the clipboard across the counter.

She reads my name then narrows her gaze on my face. Squinting, a faint smile creeps upon her mouth. "Oh, it's you?"

"Yeah." I suppress a frown.

"So, you're back?" she taunts. "Thought you'd never return."

"Not as an inmate." I raise an eyebrow. "I'm not a criminal."

"Fine. Take a seat. I'll call you back shortly."

I grab my book bag from the floor and trot over to the chairs. That bitch needs a hobby. She's so fucking sarcastic and rude.

After twiddling my thumb for several minutes, a guard summons me to the back.

I'm ushered down the hall by a short male guard. "Deja vue," I say to myself. As I get closer to Kenny's cell, the hair on the back of my neck rises. The sudden urge to run embodied me. My stomach shifts, followed by a faint ache. What is my gut telling me? I shudder forward, determined to get to the bottom of things.

The guard bangs his baton on the cell bars. Everyone stares at us. Initially, I don't see a Kenny's face. My heart drops. Then I locate him laying on a cot with his head facing the wall.

"You can meet him in a visiting room today," the guards say. "Follow me."

I give Kenny one last glance before following the officer. He hasn't moved.

Sitting in silence is driving me insane. Horrible thoughts are racing through my mind. I don't feel well. It's that sensation when a catastrophe is brewing.

The rattle of the door knob brings a quiet fear to my mind. I clench my teeth and brace myself for bad news. I'd had bad news too many times before.

Kenny enters the door. Gasping, I rise from my chair. His left eye is red and swollen, his lip busted.

I race to his side. "What happened?" I question with pain in my chest.

He turns his head. "Nothing. I got into a fight."

"That looks like more than a fight," I respond, grabbing his chin. I turn his face so I can get a better view. Anger slices through his face. I remove my hand, but my heart is heavy.

"Me and one of the shifters got into a fight. Have a seat."

I take a seat. The good news will lift his spirits.

"Did you see the news?" I question, eyes bulging.

"How? We don't have a television. I have no clue

what's going on outside these bars," he barks and rubs his eye.

"Well, another girl went missing."

He cuts me off. "How is that good news?"

"It proves you're innocent. You couldn't have kidnapped her."

"That doesn't prove anything. That proves I didn't kidnap her. It doesn't prove I didn't kill Shelly. Besides, I confessed to it."

"But I know you were forced."

"Live your life, Ronnie," he warns, his one good eye looking at me. "Forget about me."

I shake my head. "I can't forget you, Kenny. I love you." Tears fill my eyes.

"Ronnie, I will always love you." He grimaces. "When I get out in 20-30 years, we can be together. For now, go on with your life."

"I won't. I decided I'm going to go public and tell the world what Prince did to Shelly."

"Are you crazy, Ronielle?" He bangs his hand on the table. "They will come for you," he grunts.

"Who?"

"I never want to see you again. Do yourself a favor stay away from this case, you got it?" he says with a stern look. He stands from his chair. "Guard, guard, I'm ready." He walks toward the door.

"But, Kenny," I plead. I've never seen him so mad before, not directed at me. He doesn't mean what he is saying.

The guard opens the door. Kenny doesn't even say goodbye. I'm more confused than ever. I'm sure Kenny is innocent. I'm also sure that Prince is more dangerous than I initially thought.

How can I even concentrate when I'm in a state of shock? And now drops of rain flood the side walk. Lighting strikes, highlighting my path and roaring above my head. I despise rain, but lightning infatuates me. The way it whips through the clouds, not taking any shit. *One day my magic is going to be as swift and sizzling as lightening,* I think. I continue watching the clouds be struck by several bolts in a row. It's a magical show. I don't know whether to race back to campus or continue watching the show.

Reminding myself that life is one continuous rainstorm, I flip on my hood and finish walking to campus. Grandma used to say rain will come, you can either drown or dance. I danced in the rain.

However, I've always felt as if I was drowning, barely able to breathe. One disaster after another has engulfed my life.

Entering the double doors of school, I get an aroma of food. I'm not sure exactly what. Maybe chicken. My stomach growls. I'm hungry.

Stalking toward the cafeteria, I take a quick peek at the board. Tuna tar tar. I'll pass. I'm not much of a tuna girl. I'll have a sandwich and chips, which is always an alternate lunch.

Gathering my thoughts, I continue toward my room. I need to dry my hair before my next class. A jerk of my arm causes me to drop my book bag and swing. A wave of pain erupts across my arm. I don't know who it is and don't care. I don't land any punches. Mostly I'm swinging at the air. I'm not letting anyone punch me in the face. Since the entire student body hates my guts, anyone could be trying to kill me.

"Calm down," a familiar voice says. My vision is very hazy, and I'm trying to concentrate on the face.

I stop swinging and gasp, trying to catch my breath. My adrenaline is in overdrive. I try staying calm, closing my eyes. I'm fighting for my life. Flashbacks from when I was attacked by Prince bombard my thoughts, but the voice isn't his.

I open my eyes. Blinking, I narrow my vision into chestnut brown eyes. There's a grin on his face. "Josh, don't grab me like that. You know I'm on edge."

"I didn't mean to frighten you," he says while I stare at his dimples, making sure I have the right twin.

"I need to talk with you alone. In private," he urges.

"Okay," I respond. I'm slightly alarmed that I don't see James. I've always seen the two together. They are attached at the hip. "We can go to my room."

After I check my surroundings, we hurry to my room. The last thing I need is someone to catch me sneaking in another male. Boys aren't supposed to be in rooms, but no one follows that rule. Also, I don't need any slanderous gossip getting to Kenny.

Grace hasn't spent a night here in days. I'm sure she's at her boyfriend's place. No disturbances.

I slip the key into the door. That grim commotion swirls in my chest as if I'm walking into a pit of snakes. Luckily I have Josh here with me. If someone lurks in the shadows, they're in for a rude awakening. Heat hits my face as I enter. I glance over at Grace's bed, which is neatly made. She was here, left the heater running. She must watch me. She comes when I leave. Maybe to avoid the awkwardness.

"Take a seat, make yourself comfortable," I grunt before heading to the bathroom. I grab a towel from the cabinet. My hair is dripping wet.

I strut back into the room. "What's on your mind?"

"There a lot on my mind." He looks at me with such adoration. I have a thing for eyes. His brown eyes were the first thing that caught my attention. We have physical attraction, sexual tension. Problem is, I get the same sensation when I'm around James.

"But first, I have some splendid news," he claims.

"Yeah? What's that?" I cop a squat on my bed, folding one leg underneath me. I give him my undivided attention. The way he licks his lips makes my panties sizzle. Damn, I can't deny my feelings.

"I know where Prince lives."

I giggle. "That's not news." I plant my chin on my hand. "I was at his house once before. It's only a few blocks away."

"You've been to the castle?" he questions.

"Castle? I can hardly call a one bedroom loft a castle."

"What?" He shivers. "Cynthia at Mage Academy, her mom is the maid. She told me where it's located."

His words shoot through my body like hot coal. I wince at what he's going to ask next.

"Let's take an unannounced trip. You down with snooping around the castle?"

. "Sure, why not?" I respond before I can give myself a chance to think. I'm hypnotized by his seductive eyes. I stare at the shirt that clings to his sculpted abs. I've already agreed to go public. Wait, this more dangerous. What if we get caught?

His face lightens up to a glow. Without warning, he stalks toward me. I rise to my feet. My cheeks burn with passion. He kisses me and not on my cheek. It's not a friendship kiss. It's a French kiss, nice and slow. I don't want to stop.

He snatches himself away. "I'm sorry," he says. "I shouldn't have done that."

"No need to be sorry," I assure him.

"You have a boyfriend, and James likes you too."

"How long can we fight our feelings?" I question.

I figured James liked me. The feeling is mutual. Why should I choose? Everyone thinks it's okay for men to date several women.

I'll make my own rules. There are three hot guys. I will have them all.

After Josh leaves, I change into a dry uniform. Going to the castle brings in a different kind of danger. Entering someone's house is a bold move. But Josh feels that his sister is being held captive there. If that's accurate, he has limited time before she ends up dead like Shelly.

Lately, campus isn't the safest place for me either. Students are after me with no regards for law enforcement. Back home, I'd seen plenty of horrible things. Bloodshed, violence, fights. But nothing prepared me to be hunted for doing the right thing.

It's going to piss Kenny off to the max. But he has to understand. I already agreed, so I'm going to do it. Kenny and I are in a relationship and I respect his opinion. But no one owns Ronnie.

Closing the door to my dorm room brings a slice of fear. Every time I go out on campus lately, my anxiety revs up. There's no reason to be so nervous today. I'm innocent. Everyone will see. I storm down the hall to the Arts building for my next class assuming everyone will be friendly, or at least not pay me any attention. Nope, everyone is still giving me the screw face of disgust. Even though another girl went missing. I'm still guilty until proven innocent, I suppose. Another girl missing didn't change their minds. Kenny warned me this would be the outcome.

Holding my head up, I continue to my class. It's not my shame to carry anymore. I did nothing wrong. Yet I'm being isolated and crucified.

The loud chatter of the other students is refreshing. I can sneak into class, ease my butt in my chair with no one seeing me. I'm tired of being under a microscope every nanosecond.

As soon as I step in the door, there's complete silence. They were waiting for me like vultures. I'm not expecting the teacher to stand up for me. They hate me just as much as the students do.

Once I land my bottom in the chair, the chatter starts again.

Mr. Edwards bangs his ruler on the chalk board

to silence the class. He yells, "Get your textbooks out!"

Magical creatures 100 is a hard class. I don't see how it's going to help me in actual life. Mr. Edwards insists that one day you may come in contact with a creature, and you should be trained to defend yourself.

But right now, I couldn't care less about dragons and werewolf shifters. I'm more concerned about the shit storm I'm in.

"Now what will you do if a red dragon crosses your path?" Mr. Edwards questions.

"Run like a cheetah and hope he doesn't spray me with fire," David says. He's the class clown. He used to speak to me, but now he doesn't look my way.

"Ah ha, David, that would the best thing for you, since you haven't studied your lesson." Mr. Edwards turns down the collar on his shirt. His eyes glow a fluorescent orange. "But for everyone else, you stay calm and show the red dragon you're not afraid. They can sense fear and they will attack."

"So, what about a blue dragon?" Jill questions, chewing her gum like a cow. She has an oval-shaped face and a sassy attitude. She always asks the dumbest questions. If she'd shut up, we could get back to the books instead of hearing this horse shit about dragons from three centuries ago.

"The blue dragon is friendly and not a meat eater. It's unlikely that he will burn you to smithereens," Mr. Edward declares.

All this nonsense about dragons is causing my head to hurt. Mr. Edwards is overzealous with dragons. He's an ancient vampire over three hundred years old, and dragons ruled the land in his day. Now they wear suits and winged-tipped shoes. I've never seen a dragon in its authentic form.

The bell sounds. Within a second, everyone races for the door. Poor Mr. Edwards, he's still talking. I'm tired, hungry, and I can't wait to get away from the blazing, furious stares of the misfit pack.

"That bitch thinks she slick." The hot words roll off someone's tongue from behind me. If I have to guess, I'd say it's Kelly, one of the misfit pack.

Grinding my teeth and balling my fists, I continue walking. It's impossible for them to be speaking of me.

A hard shove from behind nearly knocks the wind out of me. I brace myself before I go crashing to the ground.

A muffled shriek is followed by a feminine voice. "You didn't knock her to the ground."

Whoever pushed me caught me off guard. I swivel around, swinging my fist and landing a punch into Kelly's jaw. Taniesha is the ring leader. Her bossy ass always sends the other two to do her dirty work. But Paige is not a fighter. They are turning her into a savage. I can see the fear wrinkling through her face.

I met her gaze and raise my eyebrow. She says nothing as she looks to Taniesha's hefty ass for direction.

Taniesha takes two steps forward. My mouth twists in disbelief. Standing with my arms folded, I dare her to hit me. She does just that. She slaps me so hard, she leaves a sting of pain burning on my left cheek. Mustering all the energy I have and fueled by my anger, I slap her back. I hit her with so much power, my hand buzzes. Suddenly we are in a full-on brawl. I'm being sucker punched from every direction. They're all punching me. I've been jumped before. I can handle a group of misfits.

Grabbing Paige by her blonde hair, I sling her out of my way. The other two continue throwing heavy punches. I'm holding my own until I get knocked to the ground.

My only defense while lying on the ground being attacked by two thirsty witches is my long nails.

They hover over me, pulling my hair. I claw away at someone's face. A wet substance oozes down my hands. I guess she's bleeding. I didn't care. They continue attacking, bloody face and all.

My anger is so full I almost don't notice the buzzing of my magic. It never fully blooms, only hums at the surface. I can't control it. This time the buzzing is intense and followed by a bright white light. It's electric, sizzling to the touch. Kelly and Taniesha both hop off me, howling in pain. A sheer force of the heat is burning through my hands.

I pop to my feet with my hands glowing. Yeah, bitches, come on now. Their hair is smoking. Taniesha is holding her arm, wincing in pain. Kelly's mouth is bleeding, and she has gashes across her face. Paige is crying. I walk toward them before they back away. Kelly takes off, limping her way back into the building.

Taniesha is in so much pain she can't run. I twist around and walk toward my dorm, daring one of them to touch me.

Storming into my room, I throw my book bag on the chair. Sparks of pain radiate through my body like an electrical shock. I wondered why I didn't feel any pain during the fight. I must have been working on adrenaline, but it has faded.

Limping to the bathroom, my muscles tense. A sharp pain creeps up my calf. What just happened? Tears shoot from my eyes. The pain is an intense grip. Muscles spasms. After several seconds, my muscles relax. I trip over my feet, barreling toward the bathroom. I escaped Wisconsin to get away from the drama. It seems I ran into head on at the Academy.

My bottom lip is swollen. Two searing scratches

grace my face. Three girls jumped me. My face doesn't appear that bad. Nothing that a little cocoa butter won't help. That doesn't stop the somber feeling stirring within me.

I grab my arm. It hurts the most. It's possible that it's broken. I don't care. I'm not going to the medical office on campus. I'll suffer through the pain. Tierra is a witch here that does magical healing. If the pain doesn't stop, I'll see her tomorrow. Now I need pills for the pain.

Rifling through my things, I search for some Advil. But I don't find any. Grace keeps a stash of pills. She's not here, and she won't miss two pills.

I search through the drawer of her desk, locating a bottle of oxycodone. This will take the edge off. I pop the top and push both of the pills in my mouth. I scurry over to the mini fridge and grab a bottle of coca cola.

A sudden knock brings anger and stirs it within me.

Damn. What now? I'm not going to detention or anywhere else. The misfit pack started it with me. I have a right to defend myself. I finish the can of seven up. I take my sweet, slow time to get to the door, dragging my chucks across the carpet. I know it's bullshit on the opposite side of the door. This school will find a way to make it my fault.

I can hear Headmaster Dave's voice now. *Your aggression is overshadowing your potential.*

I finally get to the door. I open it with my right hand, because my left hand is throbbing. There is Josh, standing there. I give a sheepish smile at the sight of him, followed by a groan. I grab my left arm.

"Come in," I declare, viewing the look of concern on his face.

"Are you okay?" he questions in a low tone. Low enough that I get nervous. Are the scars that hideous? Embarrassed, I want to cover my face and hide.

"Sure, I'm fine. Just a little sore," I respond.

He helps me to the bed then pulls an ice pack from his back pocket.

"I guess you heard what happened?"

He nods. Things spread through campus like wildfire. "I heard you beat the misfits' asses."

"Yeah, but they started it," I grunt. I grab the ice pack and place it on my lip.

"I know you're not a bully. Besides, you don't have to prove anything to me."

Tears fill my eyes. "I'm just so tired of everyone bullying me," I gasp, "for something I didn't do."

He walks closer and takes a seat beside me on the bed. He stares into my face with that somber expression. It strikes me like a wrecking ball: I disappointed him. I can't stop the tears.

"No, don't cry. You can't let this break you." He wipes the tears from my face. "Stay strong. Prince will be taken down. Everything will go back to normal."

He's right. I have come too far. I can't give up now. I'm going to fight to prove Kenny's and my innocence and to take down Shelly's killer if it's the last thing I do. I bury my face in his chiseled chest, not wanting him to see my scars. I take in a whiff of his scent and close my eyes, forgetting about the stress and drama of this academy. My heart rate becomes irregular. There is some sexual tension between the two of us. Again, I ponder about a sexual escapade with him.

I won't make the first move. I like to be chased. The way he caresses my back, he wants me too. I don't how much longer we can fight the temptation.

He unbuckles my bra. I lie carelessly across his chest.

He continues massaging my back. I lift my head. The look he gives me cements my beliefs. We can't control our feelings. He kisses me on the forehead then lifts my chin and brushes the tears from my face. He kisses my lips slow and soft, and I don't resist. I need him and he's a gentleman.

I lower myself onto the bed. My breathing increases in anticipation of the inevitable. I'm not nervous, I'm anxious. I'm unable to believe this is happening. I've never seen so many hot guys in one place. I've never been the pretty girl that the guys are chasing. Yet there are three guys on this campus doing just that.

His lips touch mine again. I part my lips, allowing his tongue entrance into my mouth. A thrill races down my back and I press my body harder against his. The bulge in his pants becomes larger. I can't wait to get him naked. Often, I have imagined the size of his penis. His shoe size is thirteen; I assume his penis is large.

He unbuttons his belt, and I assist him in taking his pants off. I think about safe sex. We never discussed if he was seeing someone else. I don't want to mess up the mood, but it's better safe than sorry.

"Do you have a condom?" I question, breaking our lip lock.

"Yeah, I do," he responds.

He grabs his pants and pulls a condom out. I wonder if he assumed he was getting laid or if he just carries it around. He glances at me and everything else fades away.

He puts the condom on then climbs on top. He kisses me again and my body becomes moist everywhere. My excitement is in uproar, my magic is thrumming at my fingertips.

He eases his penis in, forcing a moan to escape my lips. It's the right size for me. He whips it in and out as I beg for more. He is gentle and catering to my every need. My body burns with desire as he continues thrusting. I scream, "Yes, Josh!" I climax as my tocs curl. The experience is like heaven and my body rattles.

He doesn't stop, continuing to whip his penis into my vaginal canal. He licks my chest up to my neck, stopping at my earlobe. My legs shake with passion as he climaxes. His body stiffens as he moans and he freezes for thirty seconds.

The sex is magnificent, lasting for what seemed like an eternity.

We became one. Our bond is forever different. Crossing the line tonight is a decision I made. We can never go backwards. Being just friends isn't an option.

15

Through the roaring Chicago wind and the yelling of James and Josh arguing no one hears the rumble of the thunder clashing, warning us of the storm ahead.

"That's the address," I claim, my voice vibrating over the yelling twins. They're arguing over how we should bombard the castle.

Night has fallen upon us. Although it's not late at night, it's better than ambushing the castle in broad daylight.

It's been two days since Josh and I cemented our relationship. We decided it was best not to tell James, uncertain of his mind state and what reaction we'd get. James has expressed his feelings for me before. The feeling is mutual. But it's not the right time to address it. One day we all will be one family.

James slips into a park a few hundred feet from the entrance. I dart a glance at the massive castle. Which entrance will we sneak in? The castle is nearly as big as the school campus. There is no way we're entering the castle. Not without a guard on our ass. A grim sensation crosses my body. I dry heave, trying to catch my breath. A castle that big has guards.

"What's wrong?" James asks, rushing to my side.

Suddenly, I get a suffocating sensation. The darkness hovering around the castle sends goosebumps down my flesh. I rub my hand across my chest, trying to relieve the pressure. A nagging at the back of my mind consumes me. Natalie is in the castle. However, something more sinister and darker is present. Something that will rattle this city to its core.

The darkness of this town isn't new. I sensed it the first day I stepped off the greyhound bus. It's a town riddled with secrets that keep being swept under a rug. Prince is hiding in plain sight.

After several minutes of catching my breath, I'm calm enough to come up with a plan. I grit my teeth while eyeing the clouds. We better make this quick. It appears to be twister weather.

"What's the plan, fellas?"

"We don't need a plan. Let's just bust through the door and get Natalie," James growls.

"Calm down, James," Josh warns.

We have to think straight or we could all be dead upon entering the door. "First, how do we enter the gate?" I ask, glaring at the ten-foot steel gate.

"Well, hop the gate," Josh suggests.

"Then what? Bust through the window?" I bark.

"If we must," James responds.

"OK, we should go around back, then scale the gate and enter through the back door," Josh adds.

We are just going to snoop around. Search for clues. Natalie is inside. I can feel it in my bones. I can't bring myself to tell them what I'm sensing. I fight back my urge to urinate. It's likely fear of the unknown. What lurks behind the doors of the gloomy castle? I force myself out of the car, and the scent of decay permeates the air, masking the scent of rain.

"Do you smell that?" Josh questions.

"Yeah, I do."

James sniffs. "No, what does it smell like?"

"A rotten meat scent," Josh says, eyes bulging.

We attempt to climb the gate. I'm doing good until my shirt gets snagged and I nearly fall face first. But James catches. Wincing, I wiggle my arm. A tinge of pain pricks at my forearm. The stupid misfit pack.

"Are you okay?" Josh questions as we sneak toward the back door of the castle.

"I'm fine," I respond, not wanting him to worry about me. He needs to be focused on the grim task ahead.

James twists the knob on the door. Of course, it's locked. Why did we think we could walk to the door and open it? It is quite silly. The twins are determined to enter. Rescuing Natalie ourselves is better than calling the police.

Josh races to the side, checking all the windows. "Hey! Ronnie, James, over here," he says, snatching our attention. We scurry over to a basement window. It's cracked open. It's a skinny window, big enough for me to squeeze through, but there's no way the twins will fit.

"Ronnie, you slip through the window then open the back door for us." James orders.

The words crash and burn in my throat. I point, trembling with fear and force my words to expel. "You want me to go in alone?"

"Don't worry. We'll be right here," James insists.

Terror sweeps over me. I should say no and go back to campus. But we've come too far now. I'm risking everything. Finding Shelly's killer is worth it, I tell myself. I shoot one last glance at the twins.

"If you don't open the door in two minutes, I'm kicking it in," James assures me.

"Okay," I respond. I lower myself to the ground, then shimmy through the tiny basement window. I fall a few feet, landing in a room filled with clothes and washing appliances. I assume it's the laundry room. I stand there for a minute, making sure there are no movements. My stomach churns back and forth, rapid and hard. I almost vomit. I gather myself the begin to move through the house, quiet as a ghost.

I come upon a spiral stair case and scale the stairs until I reach the top. I'm almost holding my breath. But this house is silent, unrealistically quiet. You could hear a pin drop.

I notice an entry door at the end of the hall. This must lead to the outside. The lock makes a loud sound as I click it open. Gasping, I view darkness and a large, empty lot. Damn, is this the wrong door?

I step out the door. "Twins," I whisper. Silence is the answer I get. The plan has gone from bad to hell.

If the twins don't answer soon, I'll trample through this yard and race back to campus.

Suddenly I hear footsteps and the twins appear from the darkness.

"We have to split up. Be quiet as possible," James barks. "I'll go to the top floor. Josh, you and Ronnie take the lower level."

James likes to be the leader. Sometimes he lets his emotions get the best of him.

We split and I find my way to the massive first floor. I move silent and quick, making sure not to alarm anyone. I come upon a hall with several doors. Opening a door, I find the bathroom. No one is in here. My instincts tell me I'm close.

I find my way to the living room area. I pause for a second. I adore the chandelier and elegant furniture. Are they sure this is Prince's home? This castle must belong to a millionaire.

I stalk toward the picture-frame window. Glancing to my left, I notice pictures on the wall. One picture sticks out the most, demanding my attention. It's a picture of Headmaster Dave. My mind races a million miles. I don't understand why the headmaster's picture is in Prince's house. A thump followed by a shriek tears my attention back to the hallway. I head toward the noise when a voice sounds.

It's a feminine voice. My heart rate kicks into overdrive. I don't have a split second to think. There's more bumping, shaking the castle, causing the chandeliers to rattle. My heart hammers in my chest. I should escape. But I never listen to my instincts. Curiosity has got the better of me.

Creeping toward the hall, toward the doors, I break out in a sweat. "Hello," I whisper.

"In here." The feminine voice sounds again. Startled and terrified, I creep closer to the door. I pry the door open to find two girls, barely clinging on to life. They're emaciated, their clothes hanging from their bodies, eyes sunken with dark rings around them. Tears burn the back of my eyeballs.

"Who are you?" the taller of the two asks. I glance at the other girl closely and immediately I know it's Natalie. She resembles them down to the slim lips.

"Are you Natalie?"

"Yes," she says as she scratches her arm.

"I came with your brothers, the twins. To rescue you." I nod.

She flings her thin arms around my shoulders, gripping me tightly like death is nipping at her heels.

"Wait, there are guards," the other girl barks.

Natalie lets me out of her bear grip. Tears stream down her cheeks. "I haven't seen anyone. Trust me."

They are both fragile. I have to be strong. I'm leading them out of this hell.

I'm a ball of emotions, nervous and exited that I have found the twins' sister.

We dart through the maze of the first floor. When we're within a few hundred feet of freedom, another rumble splits the air, followed by a crash that shakes the house. The twins have run into some trouble.

We enter the kitchen and find the source of the noise. There's an all-out brawl. It's Josh and a huge guy ramming his face into the wall.

16

I must get the girls to safety, out of the ruins they have endured for the past few weeks. But my first instinct is to help Josh. The muscular dude is beating him to a pulp.

I grit my teeth and race toward them, my arms pumping at my sides. Gathering strength I didn't know I had, I kick him in the back. It's my way of warning him. Leave Josh alone.

He doesn't move a muscle. My blood freezes and my heart stops. He continues beating Josh like a drum. I grab the thing closest to me: a frying pain. I swing the pan with all the penned aggression I have in me, hitting him upside his head.

That got his attention. He stumbles to the side, releasing Josh from his grip.

He twists, his rage-filled gaze landing on my face. Fear penetrates my body. I don't move, letting him know that I'm not frightened. But I am. His bulky stature makes me flinch. My eyelids spasm. I'm on the tracks and a freight train is heading toward me. Good thing my magic is thrumming at the surface. Here he comes.

He charges toward me. I hear the two girls screaming. I want to scream too but I'm preparing for the impact.

Out of nowhere, James rushes toward him with a chair, breaking it across his head and knocking the dude to the ground. Damn, I barely dodged that bullet.

James darts on top of the dude, driving his fists into his face. I scurry to Josh's side, helping him up to his feet.

Blood trickles down his face. It brings a stream of tears to my face. I hate seeing him this way. But then he's on his feet, racing to James's side, assisting him in kicking the Incredible Hulk's ass.

When there is a pounding pain, I go falling to the ground. My head is yanked back by someone pulling my hair. Then my head is pushed down, my nose up against the floor.

"What the hell are you doing in the castle?" the

baritone voice says. The voice is unfamiliar, and it isn't Prince.

The metallic taste of blood invades my mouth, adding a bit of a rage to me. I struggle to get away from the tight grip, anger filling my mind. I force myself to concentrate. Maybe I can use my magic to free myself.

The buzz of my magic thrums through my blood. The asshole twists my head. "Who are you?" he questions as his scent fills my nostrils. It's a rather familiar, stringent scent. The same scent that floated throughout Prince's loft.

The mellow whimpers of the two girls wail in the background. "I'm Ronnie," I growl.

"What business do you have here, Ronnie?" He pushes my head harder against the floor.

I take a hard swallow. A strong bolt of magic jolts through my body, pushing the creep off me. I take in a heady breath. My breaths are quick and harsh, trying to catch up with the demands of my lungs.

There is still constant bumping, I assume from the twins fighting. My vision is hazy, but I twist my head to the side. I see the girls standing in shock, hugging each other. I try standing, but the room is spinning.

I close my eyes and force myself to a sitting position. Suddenly, a clapping noise slices through the air.

I blink repeatedly, trying to get an unobstructed view. The clap continues, followed by a male voice. "Good job, twins. You found your sister." The voice belongs to Prince. I guess this is his castle.

"You brought someone to barter with." I force my eyes open, landing my gaze on the snake's face. I stand up, my legs and hands shaky. I'm tired and exhausted, but my adrenaline is still pumping. I can't believe I was just pinned down and I used my magic. It shows up out of thin air. I have no control.

"You have returned, Ronielle," he says with a silly grin. He's wearing a golden robe, as if he is a god.

His soldiers stand at his side. The twins have migrated to Natalie. I stand face-to-face with Prince, alone. I need someone to rescue me from the outskirts of his darkness.

James steps in front of me. His shirt is ripped to shreds, and scars riddle his chest. "We have what we want. Just let us leave."

"It's not that simple. You want your sister."

He nods. "Of course."

"You can take Natalie and Tanya with you. But I keep Ronielle."

"This isn't a trade."

"Well, then Natalie goes nowhere," he says with no regards.

"Take the girls, I'll stay," I respond. The girls won't last another day. He will feed on them until they disappear.

"What? Are you sure about this?" James questions with concern.

"Yes." Fear is an understatement. This is the most fearful I've ever been. I can handle Prince. I have done it before. Will and determination are how I survive. And I have my hit-or-miss magic to protect me.

"Okay, but I stay here with Ronielle," James says.


FIND out what happens next in
   Monster light

Phantom light

Shadow light

Monster light


The Magical Jinn Series: Coming Soon

Celena's Pack Book 1

Celena's Pack Book 2

Celena's Pack Book3

Celenas's Pack Book 4

Celena's Pack Book 5


Coming Soon

Misfit Academy

Supernatural Academy

Follow me on social media

FB: facebook.com/rlwilson723

Twitter: twitter.com/exquisitenovel1

Instagram: instagram.com/rlwilson23

Tik Tok: https://vm.tiktok.com/ZMJnQnPgY/"

Join my reader group https://www.facebook.com/groups/440691789814122/

Sign-up for my newsletter https://www.subscribepage.com/f2v6g5

Check out my website
www.rlwilsonauthor.com